Walking Together

Menaqaj Pemwije'tulti'k

Elder Albert D. Marshall and Louise Zimanyi
Illustrated by Emily Kewageshig
Translated by Barbara Sylliboy and
Arlene Stevens, Eskasoni, Unama'ki

annick press
toronto • berkeley

When we walk together in a good way,
we learn to see the world
through two eyes.

We receive the gifts of Mother Earth through stories.

Menaqaj pemwije'tulti'k, etuaptmu'k Wskitqamu.

When we walk together in a good way, things are revealed.

Menaqaj pemwije'tulti'k, pana'sik kjijitaqn.

We hear those who are returning
and those who stayed
sing the Lands and Waters awake after a deep rest.

Nutu'kik apajita'jik aqq ta'n siawqatmu'tipni'k
ketapekia'tijik tukwa'tunew
Maqamikew aqq Samqwan sa'q atlasmikl.

When we walk together
in a good way on Turtle Island,
we learn we are all connected.

Menaqaj pemwije'tulti'k kmitkinaq,
kisi-kina'masulti'k msɨt newte' wejitaik.

We are never alone.
We need each other.
Mawikwayk. Together, we are strong.

Mu elam newtukwa'lukutiwk.
Nuta'yk mawo'ltinenew.
Mawikwayk. Mawikwayk, melkikna'ti'k.

When we walk together in a good way,
we learn about the gifts and stories of our family,
of the Lands, and of the Waters.

Menaqaj pemwije'tulti'k, kekina'masulti'k
iknmakwemkl aqq a'tukwaqnn ala'tu'titl kikmanaq,
wjit Maqamikew, aqq Samqwan.

Those who were here before us—
and those who will be here after us.

Ta'n eymu'tipnik ke'sk mna'q kinu—
aqq ta'nik klapis i'mu'titaq.

When we walk together in a good way,
we learn the languages of the Land.

Menaqaj pemwije'tulti'k,
kis-kina'masultitesnu tli'suti'l Wskitqamu'k.

When we walk together in a good way,
we give back gifts
by taking care of our family.

Menaqaj pemwije'tulti'k,
apaji-ika'tu'kl iknmakwemkl
maliamu'kik kikmanaq.

We leave things where they are.

Naqtmu'k koqoey ta'n tett etekɨp.

We take only if there is enough.
We ask before we take
and we listen for the answer.
We share.

Pasɨk wessua'tu'k tepiaq.
Wejikesultimk ke'sk mu wessua'tumɨt
koqoey aqq eskmatmu'k asite'lsuti.
Naskwa'tatulti'k.

We sing the Mother Earth song.
We say thank you.
Wela'lin.
Miigwech.

Elte'mu'k Wskitqamuey ktapekiaqn.
Telueyk Wela'lin.
Wela'lin.
Miigwech.

When we walk together in a good way,
we go to what we love,
we go to what we need—
Water, Stick, Rock, Frog.

When we walk together in a good way,
Frog is one of our teachers.

We wait, listen, and watch for Frog
near the ponds—
we breathe in the stillness.

Menaqaj pemwije'tulti'k,
Sqolj ekina'muksi'k.

Eskmalu'k, jilsitmakuti'k aqq jiko'taqati'k
wjit Sqolj kikjiw qospeml—
kamlamutmu'k wantaqtek.

When we walk together in a good way, things are revealed.

We hear Frog croaking.
We see Frog.
Frog watches us.
We speak Frog.

Menaqaj pemwije'tulti'k nemitu'k koqoey.

Nutu'k Sqolj mettetoqsit.
Nemiu'k Sqolj.
Sqolj jikeyuksi'k.
Sqoljewi'sulti'k.

When we walk together in a good way,
we listen to a story about Frog.
He lives in muddy water and has wrinkly skin.
He did not share the gift of flowing water
with the people and the animals.

Menaqaj pemwije'tulti'k,
jiksitmu'k a'tukwaqn wjit Sqolj.
Wikit nekm siskuapu-iktuk aqq elanqiet.
Keltɨtuasni samqwan wskwijinu'k
aqq waisisk.

Ruby-throated Hummingbird, wild Daisies, flowing River, and sunning Turtle are our teachers, too.

We'kaw Mekwi'skipat Militaw, Tskɨskl, pemitk Sipu, aqq etl-na'ku'setewa'lsit Mikjikj ekina'muksi'kik.

When we walk together in a good way,
we share wonder as we wander and play.

Menaqaj pemwije'tulti'k,
paqalaptmu'k koqoey ke'sk altaik aqq militaik.

Watching stories,
we weave and tell new stories in circle
under the Willow.

Pemaptmu'kl a'tukwaqnn,
pemitu'kl aqq aknutmu'kl kiwto'qiw
epulti'k lame'k L'mu'ji'jmnaqsi.

The stories of the Waters and the Lands and the teachings of the flyers, the crawlers, the swimmers, and the four-leggeds grow inside us.

A'tukwaqnn wjit Samqwan aqq Maqamikew aqq kina'masuti'l wejiaql alayjita'jik, alapekultijik, ali'ko'ltijik, aqq newikata'tijik etlikutikl kkamlamuninaq.

Like flossy Milkweed seeds,
they are carried on the winds
for future generations.

Nkutey,
skinaminn alsɨkl wju'sn-iktuk
wjit elmi'knikewaq.

When we walk together in a good way, we remember Mawikwayk. Together, we are strong.

When we take care of the Land and Water, the Land and Water take care of us.

Menaqaj pemwije'tulti'k, mikwite'tmu'k Mawikwayk. Toqitaik, melkikna'ti'k.

Maliaptmu'k Maqamikew aqq Samqwan, aqq Maqamikew aqq Samqwan maliamuksi'k.

Just like the braided Sweetgrass, we are stronger together.

Nkutey elisknuasikl Welim'qewe'l Msiku'l, toqa'luksi'k melkikna'ti'k.

When we walk together in a good way,
we learn to know the world through two eyes.

Menaqaj pemwije'tulti'k, kisi-etuaptmu'k wskitqamu.

Kespewa'tumk

Ewi'kmekɨp ula wi'katikn mɨta welkwija'luksiek kejiteketaq Mi'kmawaq tleyawitaq Wasoqopa'q, Nopa Sko'sia teluisitaq Saqamaw Charles Labrador, Nikana'to'q Teli-ktlamsɨtasimk aqq Nepiteketaq teluesnaq, "Ktuatqa'si, nmittesk Maskwi, Jioqsmusi aqq Kuow. Lapa'si lamqamu'k ula msɨt kmu'jk keliskentultijik. Kinu skwijinuwulti'k amujpa nkutey tela'taqati'k."

Mi'kmawiktuk, Etuaptmumk teluemk iknmakwemk milaptaqatimk, teluisik Aklasie'w-iktuk "Two-Eyed Seeing," aqq Netuklimk teluek ikatmumk Kkijinu Wksitqamu wjit kniskamijinaqi'k aqq wjit kiskukewaq wjit elmi'knikewaq. Toqa'tumk, ula klusuaqnn ekina'muksi'kl ta'n tujiw menaqaj pemwije'tulti'k , ta'n tela'taqati'k ne'kaw wela'matultimk aqq wela'sik telo'tmumk Maqamikew aqq teleyatulti'kik Msɨt Ko'kmanaq. Wksitqamuey etekl koqqwaja'taqnn aqq kinu ala'tu'kl tepkatik tela'tekemkl. Tluenes naqtmu'k Kkijinu Wksitqamu naji-klu'ktn jel mu ta'n tel-we'jitu'k.

Menaqaj Pemwije'tulti'k telitpiaq Sqoljuiku's/Sqoljik poqji-nutuj Siwk. Na tujiw jijawejk sesaqo'ltijik Unama'kik, Ewne'k miniku, Aklasie'w-iktuk teluisik Cape Breton etek No'pa Sko'sia. Tkarontok—Kmu'jk Kaqmultijik Samqwan-iktuk, Kwetejk telui'tmi'tij Toronto, na tujiw wasuekl paskasua'ql aqq nipi'jk saqatpia'tijik, ta'n tujiw apatamkiejit-iktuk nikutijik musqunamuksitjik aqq stoqnamuksitjik sa'qati'jk aqq epukjik pqojikutitaq atuomkminaqsi'k.

Kukumijinaq Tepknusetk ekinua'taqatijik ta'n tel-militpiaq na tujiw wksitqamu Kmitkinaq: a'tukwaqnn aqq aknutmaqnn wjit waisisk aqq sqaliaqnn, ta'n wettɨk wju'sn wettaqne'wasik Kniskamijinu Na'ku'set, Kaqtukaq, Kloqoejk musikiskɨtuk. A'tukwaqnn aqq aknutmaqnn piluapukwetal wije'wmi'tij ta'n tett eymn kmitkinu.

Te'sikiskɨk, ta'n pasɨk tami eymn, elta'mkl amali'ka'taqnn, kujmuk kikuaq, nipuktuk, sipuk, qospemk kisna wta'nuk, mikwite'te'n mu newtukwa'lukwewun. Jiko'teke, jiksɨtmakwe, aqq ankita'si. Koqoey wksitqamu ekina'mask wjit sqaliaqnn aqq waisisk aqq ki'l? Tal-tluek wela'lin aqq tal-kinua'tekek tel-muiwatmn kis-kina'masin?

Kinua'teke koqoey ankite'tmn aqq piltuaptmn—l'tu napuikaqn, aknutte'n, wi'ke'n aqq sesa'tu aknutmaqnml. Pipanikesi, kwilu kisa'matultioqik, aqq kwile'n pilui-kjitekemk ewe'wmn kpukikl.

AWJIT ULA MAWLUKUTIMK

Ta'n tujiw nuta'q tapusijik wenik toqwa'tinew, toqwa'titaq. Ta'n tujiw wen nemituaj telqamiksilitl pilue'l aqq ketu'-nenuatl mɨta kejitoq wja'tuatew wantaqo'ti aqq ketlewo'qn. Mu mektmuwk ta'n tel kisi-tla'sik. Wesua'tu'k aqq kepmite'tmu'k tel-mawita'yk. —Kisiku Albert D. Marshall

WJIT L'NUI'SUTI'L

Tetuji keknue'k ikaik teli'sulti'k, amujpa teli-wsua'tu'k maqamikew nkutey ekina'muksi'kek aqq siaw kina'masulti'k kisna il-kina'masulti'k ta'n kjijaqamijinaq, kkamlamuninal, ktinininal aqq telita'sulti'k teli-wettaqne'wasulti'k Maqamikek. Ke'sk ula Mawikwajik Te'sunemiksijik Kisutmi'tip Metlasipunqekl L'nui'suti Keknuite'tasiktn Wksitqamu'k (2022 -2032) amujpa wiaqa'tasik teli-apa'ja'tu'k tli'suti'minu mɨta tli'suti'minu aqq kjijitaqnn wettaqne'wasikl Maqamikek.

Afterword

We wrote this story together inspired by the wisdom of the late Mi'kmaq Spiritual Leader and Healer Chief Charles Labrador of Acadia First Nation, Nova Scotia who said, "Go into the forest, you see the Birch, Maple, Pine. Look underground and all those trees are holding hands. We as people must do the same."

In Mi'kmaq, Etuaptmumk means the gift of multiple perspectives also known as Two-Eyed Seeing, and Netukulimk means protecting Mother Earth for the ancestors and for present and future generations. Together, these words teach us that when we walk together in a good way, our actions are always in harmony and balance with the Land and All Our Relations. Nature has rights and we have responsibilities. This means we leave Mother Earth a better place than we found it.

Walking Together takes place during Spring, during Squoljuiku's/Frogs Croaking Time Moon. In Unama'ki, Land of the Fog, also known as Cape Breton, Nova Scotia, this is the time when the peepers are active. In Tkaronto—Trees Standing in Water, also known as Toronto, it is the time of flowers blooming and budding leaves, when the Tamarack trees are growing their blue-green needles and the delicate white flowers of the strawberry plants will soon appear.

The Grandmother Moons describe what is happening in nature at that time across Turtle Island: the stories of animal and plant life, the different winds connected to Grandfather Sun, the Thunder Beings, and the Stars in the sky. The stories will be different depending on what Lands you are on.

Everyday, wherever you are, in a park, in your backyard, in the forest, at a river, lake, or ocean, know that you are never alone. Watch, listen, and wonder. What is nature teaching you about the plants and the animals and about yourself? How can you say thank you and show your gratitude?

Share your wonder and curiosity—draw, tell, write, and share your stories. Ask questions, build relationships, and look for different ways to know through your two eyes.

ABOUT THE COLLABORATION

Whenever there is a need for two energies to connect, they will come together. It's the ability of an individual to detect a certain energy that brings peace and openness to get to know this person. We do not question how it was meant to happen. We accept it and honor how we came together. —Elder Albert D. Marshall

A NOTE ON INDIGENOUS LANGUAGES

At this critical juncture, we need to embrace Land as teacher and continue to (re)learn our connection to and with the Land through spirit, heart, mind, and body. During this United Nations Decade of Indigenous Languages (2022–2032) this has to be part of language revitalization as our languages and wisdoms are from the Land.

MI'KMAQ PRONOUNCIATIONS

Walking Together – Menaqaj Pemwije'tulti'k
Men-ahk-hah-j Bemu-gee-ay dool-deeg

Mother Earth – Wskitqamu
Oog-sit-gah-moo

Etuaptmumk – the gift of multiple perspectives
Eh-doo-aph-duh-mumk

Land – Keskaqmikek
Ges-gah-mee-gayk

Water – Samqwan
Sam-gwann

Together, we are strong. – Mawikwayk.
Ma-wee-gwyg

Gifts – Iknmatultimkl
Iggen-imma-dool-dimk-el

Story – Wta'tukwanm (his/her)
Ooh-dah dook-wan-um

Thank you – Wela'lin
Wil-lah-len

Stick – Kmu'j
Guh-mooj

Rock – Kune'tew
Goon-eh-dew

Frog – Sqolj
Skolch

Hummingbird – Militaw
Mill-ee-daw

Daisies – Tskiskl
Disk-isk-uhl

Turtle – Mikjikj
Mig-jig-itch

Sweetgrass – Welima'qewe'l
Well-ee-muh geh-wail

To co-exist with the land; take enough, but never too much; protect Mother Earth for current and future generations – Netukulimk
Neh-doo-goo-limbk

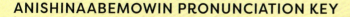

ANISHINAABEMOWIN PRONUNCIATION KEY

Thank you – Miigwech
Meeg-wetch

Wjit ta'n wenik Kis-wi'kmi'tij aqq Kisitu'titl Napuikaqnn

Kisi-wasoqatesteket: Nadine Lefort

Kisiku Albert D. Marshall, wesko'tk Espa'lsutiey Wi'katikn wjit Knukwatiknn aqq Nikanpukuit Teli-ktlamsitasimk wjit Mi'kmaq, wetapeksit Tia'm Wtutemk Mi'kmaq. Wikit Eskisoqnik—ta'n pikwelkik stoqnk etlikutijik—Unama'kik Ewne'k Miniku (Cape Breton), No'pa Sko'sia, Mi'kmaqWmitkiwew. Kisite'tkɨp Etuaptekemk (Two-Eyed Seeing)—teluemk newte'jkkpukik ewe'wmumk nmitunew ta'n tetuji-mlkiknaq ankaptasik mimajuaqnaqq mimajimk ewe'wmumk L'nui-kjijitaqn aqq L'nuey kejitekemkeweyaqq ktik kpukik ewe'wmumk nmitunew ta'n tetuji-mlkiknaq ankaptasikmimajuaqn aqq mimajimk ewe'wmumk Qame'kewey kjijitaqn aqq Qame'kewey kejitekemkewey—aqq maw-keknue'k kɨtk kpukikinal ewe'wmnew kulaman nentesnu iknmakwemkl mesnmu'kl aqq ta'n tepkatiktla'taqatinew wjit Msɨt Ko'kmanaq, aqq Kkijinu Wksitqamu.

Mawi-ksatmap ketuatqa'si nipuktuk, l'pa tetuji wl-kwija'luek. Kisi-pekaji-aknutman wlo'ti nekmeweyiktis, ta'n tujiw eymn nipuktuk mu koqoey jipatmu'n, l'pa tel-wlqatmn kutey kikuaq i'mnek. Welkwija'luek aqq nepitekek aqq iljo'qa'lɨsk.

Kisi-wasoqatesteket: Peony Birch

Louise Zimanyi, wetapeksitjik Wenuj aqq Hungarianaq, wunijanit, nuji-kina'muet espikina'matnewo'kuo'm, aqq pipanuijket, wikit aqq etl-papit Tkaronto—Kmu'jk kaqamultijik Sam'qwan-iktuk (Toronto), wettaqne'wasik Ankukamkewey 13 aqq Wmitkiwew Kisa'matultimk teluisik Newte'jit Eptaqn aqq Newte'jit Emqwanji'j. Pipanuijkatk ta'n tel-kina'muemk aqq tela'taqatimk wjit Wksitqamu atel poqji-kina'masimk apoqntɨtew Netuklimk wjit kikmanaq kiskukaqq elmi'knik wije'wmumkl menaqaj tela'matultimk aqq mawi-apoqnmatultimk.

Nutqweyaney koqoey mawi-ksatmap tel-lukwey kwijmuk na ela'timk qasqe'k: mekwe'k aqq wape'k tekismimkeweym, sankew-mila'timk atuomk-iktuk, sam'qwan, sike'saqnawk, kun'tal, aqq kmu'ji'jl, ali'ko'ltimk eymi'tij tku'k aqq kwijmuk etlatalumk.

Kisi-wasoqatesteket:
Shelby Andrews

Emily Kewageshig na Anishnaabe nuji-amaliteket aqq a'tukwet ewe'wkl napuikaqnn, wtlukwaqnk nemitumk tel-mawtaqne'wasik koqoey mimajik ewe'wkl kitk sa'qewe'l aqq kiskukewe'l kisitaqne'l aqq tel-we'wasik. Kisitoql amalitaqnn nemitumk L'nui-kjijitaqn aqq telo'ltimkewey. Emily tleyawit Saugeen L'nue'kati etek Ontario, Kanata.

Ta'n tujiw kwilm wantaqo'ti aqq wlo'ti te's apaja'si nipuktuk. Ni'n aqq nkwis Lawson welqatmek te'sikiskikl alatqieyek, majulkwatmekl waisisk jilaptu'tijik, mawo'tuekl kun'tal ankua'tunen kisi-mawte'mekl aqq pasik iloqaptmnen tetuji wulamu'k na'ku'set walqwasiet Qospem Huron. Wksitqamuey mimajua'luksiek aqq ne'kaw weji-kina'masiek aqq iapjiw mu'iwatesnen nekmewey.

Arlene Stevens Tleyawit Eskisoqnik, Unama'ki, No'pa Sko'sia, Etl-lukwet Essissoqnikewey Siawa'sik-l'nuey Kina'matnewo'kuo'm (Eskasoni Immersion School) kiwaskiwi'kiket aqq elukwatk Mi'kmawi'simkewey kekina'muemk aqq nikana'toq Mi'kmawey nujintu'timk wjit Holy Family Parish Alasutmo'kuo'm, Eskisoqnik aqq pilue'l L'nue'kati'l etekl tepow.

Barbara Sylliboy kaqi-lukwep wjit Eskasoni School Board ki's newipunqekl. L'nu'-kina'muep Eskisoqnik Kina'matnewo'kuo'm aqq elt etl-lukwep Essissoqnikewey Siawa'sik-l'nuey Kina'matnewo'kuo'm (Eskasoni Immersion School) kiwaskiwi'kiket aqq elukwatk Mi'kmawi'simkewey kekina'muemk etek Eskisoqnik, Unama'ki, No'pa Sko'sia. Katu me' pem-na'tal-lukwet kiwaskiwi'kiket aqq naspitl milamu'kl mawaknutmamkl apoqntmn tli'suti aqq ta'n telo'ltimk aqq kina'muen koqoey kisi-kina'masit telipkitawsit.

About the Authors and Illustrator

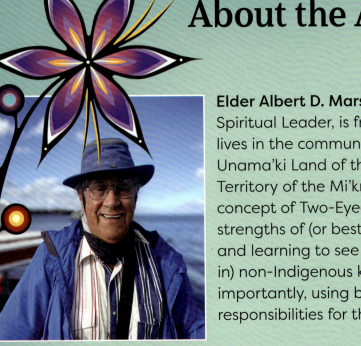

Photo credit: Nadine Lefort

Elder Albert D. Marshall, Honorary Doctor of Letters and Mi'kmaq Spiritual Leader, is from the Moose Clan of the Mi'kmaq Nation. He lives in the community of Eskasoni—*where the fir trees are plenty*—in Unama'ki Land of the Fog (Cape Breton), Nova Scotia, the Traditional Territory of the Mi'kma'ki. He has been working to bring forward the concept of Two-Eyed Seeing—learning to see from one eye with the strengths of (or best in) Indigenous knowledges and ways of knowing, and learning to see from the other eye with the strengths of (or best in) non-Indigenous knowledges and ways of knowing—and most importantly, using both of these eyes together to know your gifts and responsibilities for the benefit of All Our Relations, for Mother Earth.

My favorite moments were to just go and be in the woods, you just get a wonderful feeling. If you could explain happiness, when you are in the forest nothing scares you, you feel so at home. A place of comfort and healing and to restore balance.

Photo Credit: Peony Birch

Louise Zimanyi, of French-Canadian and Hungarian descent, is a mother, professor, and researcher and lives, works, and plays in Tkaronto—Trees Standing in Water (Toronto), part of Treaty 13 and the Dish with One Spoon territory. She explores how Earth-centered pedagogy and practice in the early years can plant the seeds of sustainability for current and future generations through respectful relationships and reciprocity.

My favorite outdoor play memories when I was young were at the beach: my red bathing suit with white piping, slow play with sand, water, shells, rocks, and sticks, swimming in waves, and picnic lunches.

Photo credit: Shelby Andrews Photography

Emily Kewageshig is an Anishnaabe artist and visual storyteller whose work captures the interconnection of life forms using both traditional and contemporary materials and methods. She creates artwork that highlights Indigenous knowledge and culture. Emily is from Saugeen First Nation in Ontario, Canada.

When I am searching for the feeling of peace and happiness I always return to the forests. My son Lawson and I have enjoyed spending so many of our days hiking, following animal tracks, collecting rocks for our growing collection, and taking in the beautiful Lake Huron sunsets. Nature makes us feel the most alive and always has something new to teach us, and for that we are forever grateful.

Arlene Stevens lives in Eskasoni, Cape Breton, Nova Scotia, where she works as a translator and Mi'kmaw language curriculum builder for the Essissoqnikewey Siawa'sik-I'nuey Kina'matnewo'kuo'm (Eskasoni Immersion School) and leads the Mi'kmaw choir at the Holy Family Parish Church, Eskasoni and the surrounding Mi'kmaw communities.

Barbara Sylliboy is a retired Mi'kmaw educator who worked as a language teacher and Mi'kmaw language curriculum builder for the immersion school in her community of Eskasoni, Cape Breton, Nova Scotia. She continues to keep busy as a Mi'kmaw language translator and sits on various advisory boards to share her language and life experiences.

To our past, present, and future knowledge holders.
—Elder Albert D. Marshall

To all who carry, create, tell, and inspire stories through their words
and art . . . the world needs more storytellers and listeners.
—Louise Zimanyi

To Lawson.
—Emily Kewageshig

© 2025 Elder Albert D. Marshall and Louise Zimanyi (text)
© 2025 Emily Kewageshig (illustrations)

First published in English by Annick Press in 2023.

Translated into Mi'kmaq by Barbara Sylliboy and Arlene Stevens, Eskasoni First Nation, Unama'ki (Cape Breton), Nova Scotia
Cover art by Emily Kewageshig, designed by Marijke Friesen
Interior designed by Marijke Friesen

Edited by Stephanie Strachan and Mary Beth Leatherdale

Annick Press and its logo are registered trademarks of Annick Press Ltd.

Annick Press supports the copyright of the creators of this work. As readers buying authorized editions of this book and complying with copyright law you do likewise. All rights are reserved without the permission of the copyright holder and publisher. These uses include reproducing, storing, training, retrieving, and transmitting in any form including electronic, mechanical, photocopying, recording, or otherwise. Distributing this work online is illegal and punishable by law. Your support of the creators of this work is appreciated.

This book is funded in part by the Government of Canada. *Ce livre est financé en partie par le gouvernement du Canada.* We acknowledge the support of the Canada Council for the Arts. *Nous remercions le Conseil des arts du Canada de son soutien.* We would like to acknowledge the funding support of the Ontario Arts Council (OAC) and the Government of Ontario for their support. We also acknowledge the support of the Government of Ontario through the Ontario Book Publishing Tax Credit, and through Ontario Creates.

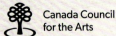    

Library and Archives Canada Cataloguing in Publication

Title: Walking together = Menaqaj pemwije'tulti'k / written by Elder Albert D. Marshall and Louise Zimanyi ; illustrated by Emily Kewageshig.
Other titles: Menaqaj pemwije'tulti'k
Names: Marshall, Albert (Albert D.), author. | Zimanyi, Louise, author. | Kewageshig, Emily, illustrator. | Sylliboy, Barbara, translator. | Stevens, Arlene, translator. | Container of (work): Marshall, Albert (Albert D.). Walking together. | Container of (expression): Marshall, Albert (Albert D.). Walking together. Micmac.
Description: Translated by Barbara Sylliboy and Arlene Stevens. | Text in original English and in Mi'kmaw translation.
Identifiers: Canadiana (print) 20250113589 | Canadiana (ebook) 20250113635 | ISBN 9781834020174 (hardcover) | ISBN 9781834020198 (EPUB) | ISBN 9781834020204 (PDF)
Subjects: LCSH: Human ecology—Juvenile literature. | LCSH: Traditional ecological knowledge—Juvenile literature. | CSH: Mi'kmaq—Juvenile literature. | LCGFT: Picture books. | LCGFT: Creative nonfiction.
Classification: LCC GF48 .M37165 2025 | DDC j304.2—dc23

Published in the U.S.A. by Annick Press (U.S.) Ltd.
Distributed in Canada by University of Toronto Press.
Distributed in the U.S.A. by Publishers Group West.

Printed in China

annickpress.com